Dedicated to the crews of
the USS Iowa
1943-1949
1951-1958
1984-1990
And the Battleship Iowa
Museum, established 2012

www.mascotbooks.com

Vicky! Mascot First Class of the USS Iowa

All pictures are courtesy of the Pacific Battleship Center.
Author Photo Credit: Jim Gauderman

For more information, please contact:
Mascot Books
620 Herndon Parkway #320
Herndon, VA 20170
info@mascotbooks.com

Library of Congress Control Number: 2019906942

CPSIA Code: PRT0719A
ISBN-13: 978-1-64307-373-6

Printed in the United States

Vicky!

Mascot First Class of the USS Iowa

Written by Mike and Carole Hershman

Illustrated by Alaina Luise

Captain John McCrea with Vicky aboard the USS Iowa

In 1943 Captain John McCrea brought his little dog Vicky on the brand new battleship, the USS Iowa. Vicky was a boy dog and his real name was Victory. Everyone called him Vicky. Sometimes they spelled it "Vickie" or "Vickey," but they loved their little dog. Even the President of the United States loved Vicky.

This is Vicky's story...

When Vicky came aboard the USS Iowa, he had to complete all of the sailor's paperwork. He was issued a photo I.D. and even completed a swimming test.

SWIM TEST

DATE: 05/06/43
SAILOR: VICTORY
RANK: MASCOT
SUPERVISOR:

500 METER:
LAPS COMPLETED:

UNDERWATER
DISTANCE: ENDURANCE:

APPROVED?

SUPERVISO

Vicky tried to learn the sailor's jobs,
but some were hard for a little dog.

Paint, paint, paint the big metal mushroom!

OOPS!

Vicky often took a nap in the nearest sailor's bunk he could find.

Near the end of his time on the USS Iowa, he even got caught and written up for it.

OOPS!

One day Vicky was up on the bow of the Iowa when he spotted a big seal on a red buoy and started barking.

MASCOT VICTORY!

REPORT TO THE BRIDGE!

As soon as Vicky climbed back on the dock and ran up the Iowa's ramp, he heard the loudspeakers.

Vicky knew he was in trouble and ran up the ladders to the bridge. He knew Captain McCrea would be waiting.

"Vicky, I have a very important job that only you can do. The President of the United States is going to be our guest for fifteen days on a very important mission. I know he will miss his dog Fala, and I want you to play with him like Fala does."

"Yes sir!" Vicky barked.
He wasn't in trouble after all.

On November 12, 1943, the USS Iowa and Vicky welcomed a new passenger aboard the ship. Franklin D. Roosevelt, the President of the United States, came up a special ramp (sailors call a "brow") from the USS Potomac.

In those days presidents often had their own private yachts.
The Potomac had a bathtub and an elevator. The USS Iowa
installed two elevators and a bathtub for the President's trip.

"John, who is this little dog?

"He's Vicky, Mr. President. Our ship's mascot."

"Where does the dog sleep?"

Later in the Captain's Cabin, President Roosevelt wanted to see if Vicky could perform all of Fala's favorite tricks.

"Roll over, Vicky!" the President said. Vicky rolled over and smiled. The President smiled too.

Vicky liked to nap on the President's lap in the Captain's Cabin.

He also loved sleeping at night with the President in the Captain's Bedroom.

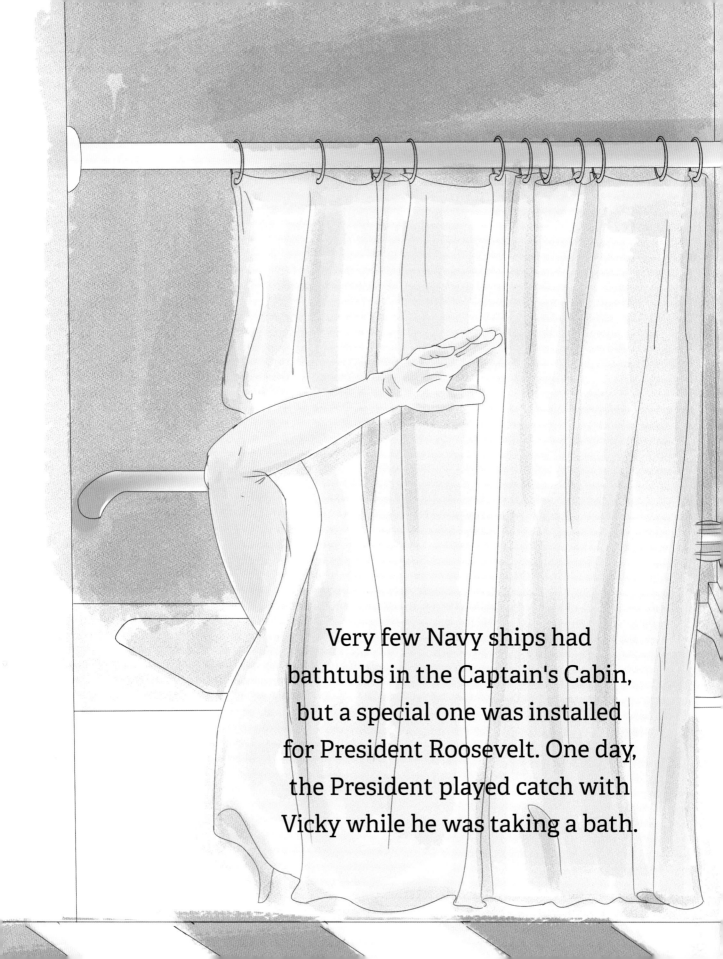

Very few Navy ships had
bathtubs in the Captain's Cabin,
but a special one was installed
for President Roosevelt. One day,
the President played catch with
Vicky while he was taking a bath.

The President's time on the USS Iowa went by so fast, and soon it was time for him to go home. Before he left, he spoke to the crew on the back of the ship...

"Captain McCrea, officers and men of the Iowa...I have had a wonderful trip on the Iowa, one I shall never forget...From all I can see and all I have heard, the Iowa is a happy ship and having served in the Navy for many years, I know, and you know what that means... And so goodbye for a while. I hope I will have another cruise on this ship. Meanwhile, good luck, and remember that I am with you in spirit, each and every one of you."

-Franklin D. Roosevelt
December 16, 1943

President Roosevelt never sailed on the USS Iowa again.

On January 30, 1949, Mascot First Class Victory was given full honors as he left the USS Iowa for the last time after over five years of service. He was going to rejoin his old friend Captain (now Vice Admiral) McCrea. A speech honoring Vicky was read!

"...as a member of the crew of the USS Iowa, you have through your devotion to duty...maintained a high moral standing toward your shipmates."

Vicky never sailed on the USS Iowa again either, but he was always proud of the time he served on the ship.

Here are some service records from Vicky's time on the USS Iowa

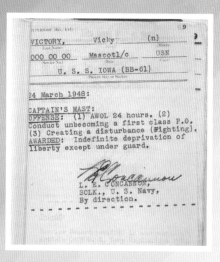

UNITED STATES NAVY
IDENTIFICATION CARD

VICTORY, Vickey (n)
NAME
/s/ Vickey (n) Victory
SIGNATURE
COLOR HAIR Tan & Brown   EYES Grey
WEIGHT 18   BIRTH 11-11-
VOID AFTER 3-23-51
L. E. CONCANNON, SCLK, U.
000 00 00

Vicky's I.D. card

VICTORY,   Vicky   (n)
000 00 00   Mascot1/c   USN
U. S. S. IOWA (BB-61)

24 March 1948:

CAPTAIN'S MAST:
OFFENSE: (1) AWOL 24 hours. (2)
Conduct unbecoming a first class P.O.
(3) Creating a disturbance (fighting).
AWARDED: Indefinite deprivation of
liberty except under guard.

L. E. CONCANNON,
SCLK., U. S. Navy,
By direction.

Vicky getting in trouble on board
the ship!

I am VICKY (short for VICTORY), Mascot
First Class, U.S. Navy
I am enroute from Hong Kong, China to
Washington, D.C. to 'retire' after seven
years continuous service at sea in the
battleship IOWA and the destroyer RUPER
I am a veteran of WW II having had wa
service in the Atlantic, Mediterranean,
Central Pacific, South Pacific & Wester
Pacific. I took part in the operations a
Kwajalien, Eniwetok, Saipan, Guam, Truk,
Western New Guinea, Western Carolines,
Leyte, Second Battle of the Philippines
Iwo Jima, Okinawa and Japan. I was the
first American dog to land in Japan at
(see reverse side)

the end of the War and was in Tokyo Bay
for the surrender ceremonies.
If I am found wandering loose and los
please take me into custody and telegra
collect (after 15 December) my whereab
to Captain L.C. QUIGGLE, USN, Care of
Colonel Villavet, U.S.A., 4420 36th St.
N.W., Washington, D.C. He will arrange
for my shipment to Washington. I have h
rabies vaccinations.
It is hoped that I do not get lost as
This tag is a precaution to help locate
if I should.

Vicky's dog tags

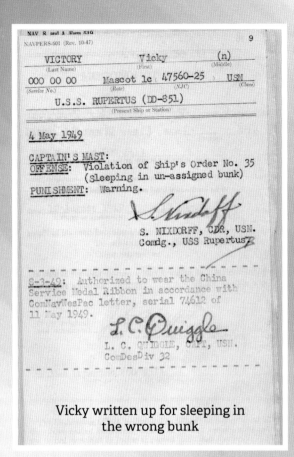

VICTORY   Vicky   (n)
(Last Name)   (First)   (Middle)

000 00 00   Mascot 1c   47560-25   USN
(Service No.)   (Rate)   (NJC)   (Class)

U.S.S. RUPERTUS (DD-851)
(Present Ship or Station)

4 May 1949

CAPTAIN'S MAST:
OFFENSE: Violation of Ship's Order No. 35
(Sleeping in un-assigned bunk)
PUNISHMENT: Warning.

S. NIXDORFF, CDR, USN.
Comdg., USS Rupertus

5-1-49: Authorized to wear the China
Service Medal Ribbon in accordance with
ComNavWesPac letter, serial 74612 of
11 May 1949.

L. C. QUIGGLE, CAPT, USN.
ComDesDiv 32

Vicky written up for sleeping in
the wrong bunk

VICTORY.   Vicky   (n)
000 00 00   Mascot 1c   USN
U.S.S. IOWA (BB61)

29 March 1943: Qualified in recruit swimming test "C".
Ability to swim 50 yards, to tread water
with ordinary attire on. Will also retrieve
sticks.

11-27-43: Duly initiated into the Royal
Order of Shellbacks, having crossed the
equator this date.

11-28-43: The essential benefits of NSLI
have been explained to this canine, and he
has stated that he does no desire to make
application for same.

6-25-45: Authorized to wear Philipine
Liberation Ribbon with two (2) bronze stars
for service in U.S.S. IOWA (BB61) during
period 17 October 1944 to 21 December 1944,
inclusive. Authority: AlNav 64-45.

8-27-45: Received the commendation as a
member of Task Force 31 and the Occupation
Force of the Japanese Homeland, Tokio Area,
and being the first American Dog on the
Japanese Empire Soil, (to the best of our
knowledge).

1-21-46: Crossed the 180th Meridan on this
date at latitude ---- and qualified to enter
the Realm of the Golden Dragon.

16 August 1945: Advanced to Mascot First
Class this date. Auth: BuDogs Bark ltr.
00555 of 8-16-45.

Certified to be correct:

L.E. CONCANNON, SCLK, USN.,
Personnel Officer.

Notes from Vicky's swim test

---

10   EACH ENTRY MUST BE DATED

VICTORY   Vicky
000 00 00   First Class   47560-22
U.S.S. IOWA (BB61)

7-18-47:

Completed the Dog Training Course and
practical lessons for Chief Mascot with
a mark of B.O. Not recommended to Rupertus
this date to take examination for Chief
since combinations not requested.

J. GOODEN,
Officer, U. S. Navy.
By direction of C.O.

7-1-48:

Service Record verified in accordance with
Article 0803 U. S. Navy Regulations 1948.

EACH ENTRY MUST BE DATED   9

NAME (Last)   (First)   (Middle)
VICTORY,   Vicky   (n)
SERVICE NO.   RATE Mascot   NJC   CLASS
00 000 00   First Class   47560-22   USN
PRESENT SHIP OR STATION
U. S. S. IOWA (BB61)

1-30-49

"As a plank-owner and member of the crew
of the U.S.S. IOWA for the past six years,
you have performed your duty as Mascot
First Class in an outstanding manner. In
war and peace you have exhibited all those
sterling qualities expected of " A Man's
Best Friend". Loyal, courageous, and
cheerful, you have contributed substantial-
ly to the morale of the ship. The Captain,
officers, and the entire crew regret your
departure and wish you well in your new
assignment." "Well Done".

B. M. DODSON,
Commander, U. S. Navy,
Commanding.

Vicky's final service record

Author's Note

Franklin D. Roosevelt came on board the Iowa on November 12, 1943, and was transported across the Atlantic Ocean to North Africa where he boarded a plane to Cairo, Egypt, for the Cairo Conference. He then flew on to Tehran, Iran, for the Tehran Conference. While he was gone, the Iowa steamed back across the Atlantic to Bahia, Brazil, and then back again to West Africa where the ship picked up Roosevelt for the return trip home. He boarded the ship from a French destroyer using a Boatswain's chair suspended from a rope rather than the brow (ramp) used to board from the Potomac.

FDR's farewell speech on the USS Iowa

Vicky stayed with the Iowa until 1949 when the ship was decommissioned. During that time, he traveled over 205,000 miles, received numerous battle ribbons, and was the first American dog to land in occupied Japan.

After his trip on the Iowa, Franklin D. Roosevelt made at least two more sea voyages aboard naval ships. He traveled on the USS Quincy to the Yalta Conference and the USS Baltimore for a conference with Admiral Nimitz and General Douglas MacArthur at Pearl Harbor. Fala accompanied him on the USS Baltimore and was known to visit sailors in their bunk areas for treats.